D0515656

# The Monsters' Picnic

By Liza Alexander
Illustrated by Joe Ewers

A SESAME STREET/GOLDEN PRESS BOOK
Published by Western Publishing Company, Inc.,
in conjunction with Children's Television Workshop.

This educational book was created in cooperation with the Children's Television Workshop, producers of SESAME STREET. Children do not have to watch the television show to benefit from this book. Workshop revenues from this product will be used to help support CTW educational projects.

It was that time of year again. Time for the Monsters' Picnic!

But not just any day would do. The day for the Monsters' Picnic had to be perfect. There had to be a warm sun, a whispering wind, and tulips in bloom. Herry Monster was in charge of knowing when the time was right.

Every day Herry looked carefully at the tulips in his window box. One morning he had a hunch that the next day the tulips would bloom.

"There's no time to waste," thought Herry. "Today there's a warm sun and a whispering wind. Tomorrow might be the perfect day for the picnic." Herry ran out to Sesame Street to spread the word.

Monsters all over Sesame Street dropped everything to get ready.

Marilyn Monster made monster-mashed-potato salad.

Malcolm and Monya Monster mixed up some monsterade.

Marvin Monster dug his monster-ball set out of his closet.

Mabel and Max Monster washed and waxed the monster bus.

The next morning Herry rushed to his window box.
The tulips were in bloom!

Herry dashed outside. The warm sun was shining! He lifted his thumb to the breeze and felt it tickle his fur. "The whispering wind!" yelled Herry joyfully. "Today is the day!"

*"Ur-roog!"* He honked his special horn, and the monsters piled into their bus and were off!

After a long drive out into the country, the monster bus
screeched to a stop. A path led up a hill to a glade bright
with tulips for the Monsters' Picnic. Monsters tumbled out
of the bus and scrambled up the hill.

*"Ur-roog!"* Herry honked his horn and announced, "Let the monster games begin!"

The monsters played monster in the middle, monster steps, and monster tag.

Some monsters played monster ball and blind monster's buff. Other monsters sat in a shady spot and played sit-down games.

*"Ur-roog!"* Herry honked his horn. "Friends, it's time to eat!"

The monsters spread out their picnic lunch. They slurped monsterade and munched on monster-mashed-potato salad. They chomped on sandwiches of monster mayonnaise and mangos.

As the monsters roasted marshmallows for dessert a giant black cloud rolled across the sun. Rumble! Rain gushed down on the glade. Soaked and frenzied monsters scurried to the monster bus for shelter.

"Oh, dear," said Herry. "It's not supposed to rain on the day of the Monsters' Picnic."

With their noses pressed against the windows of the bus, the monsters watched as the black cloud rolled away. It took the rain with it, and once again the sun shone brightly.

*"Ur-roog!"* Herry Monster honked his horn and said, "Let's not let a little rain spoil our lovely day!" Then Herry began to dance.

One by one the monsters joined in the dancing. They stomped their feet on the wet ground and waved their arms as the warm sun dried their fur. The monsters twirled and jumped and yodeled!

Marilyn Monster grabbed Herry's horn. *"Ur-roog!"*

"Fellow monsters," she announced, "this has been the best picnic day ever. What do you say?"

"Hip-hip-hurray!" yelled the monsters.

"We have the warm sun, there's a whispering wind, and the tulips are in bloom," said Marilyn. "And next year let's have a brief, refreshing rain shower, too."

"Hear, hear!" the monsters cried.

Then as tulips waved in the whispering wind, everybody joined paws in a circle. The picnic ended as the monsters danced joyfully beneath the warm sun.